DIRTY MAID

DIRTY BILLIONAIRE BOSS

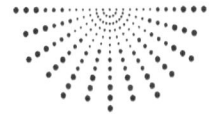

TALA MELTON

plicit Press
Erotica Fiction

GET NAUGHTY UPDATES

Click here or Visit
TalaMelton.com
for more Naughty Maid Stories

Dirty Maid: Dirty Billionaire Boss

Digital Edition 1 is Copyright © 2020 by Tala Melton. All rights reserved.

eISBN: 978-1-62327-706-2

Print ISBN: 978-1-62327-707-9

CHAPTER ONE

*T*he house was really much larger than the four bedrooms, three bathrooms from the agency briefing. It was also incredibly messy for one person. It was Friday, and Duwayne Jones, *billionaire playboy extraordinaire*, was having one of his *unplanned, not quite parties* later that evening, so he didn't really have the time to orientate his new maid, Julia, with the ins and outs of his lifestyle. She would have to hit the ground running, and the pace promised to be hectic.

"The agency said that this was your first job," he asked the 23-year old with the *too black* hair.

"Yes... But I have a lot of experience cleaning!" Julia was trying to sell herself even though she already had the job.

"No, that's perfect. So you won't have any preconceptions. I like someone blind because things can get a little messy. It will help if you don't have anything to compare it to..."

"Okay..." She was looking around the messy kitchen. The living room was also in a state. She'd only just heard about the *intimate* gathering that evening, so she really needed to get started. She watched Mr. Jones for a minute, waiting to be released, needing it actually, but he just seemed to want to look at her a minute longer. At last, he told her to carry on, his mobile phone ringing.

It took forever to get the house barely presentable. It was almost 8 PM when she eventually got to his bedroom, having already set up drinks and snacks downstairs for the 8 or *20* people Duwayne hinted might come through. His bedroom was *ground zero*, messier than the whole house combined. Duwayne was nothing like she expected a billionaire to be. She thought that this mess wasn't all his, but how one could make the money that he obviously made from this mess was beyond her.

Julia's hair had been in a bun all day, but now it was in a loose ponytail. She was looking almost as disheveled as the mess she was now cleaning, picking up clothes and underwear that clearly belonged to Mr. Jones. All except one piece that is, quite obviously, a woman's. She was holding this piece of apparel when he walked in.

"Downstairs looks great..." he said, startling her.

"Thank you... I'll be done in a minute up here, or I could give you space to get ready?" She felt like she knew him, already, just from cleaning up his mess.

"It's fine..." he said, already shirtless. He pulled his trousers off and put a towel around his waist over his underwear. He walked into his bathroom, shouting back into the room, "You can sort this out tomorrow. Call it a night!"

She stood in the room, still holding the piece of underwear for which she got no explanation. Of course, she wasn't going to get an explanation. She was just there to clean, stay quietly out of the way, and clean some more. Now she could go to her room and have her own much-needed shower.

Julia finished picking up all the clothes and made the bed. Then she went downstairs and dropped the laundry in the machine, turning it on before she went through the side door that got her to her own small courtyard. Her room was small and comfortable and everything that she needed. It really was more than she needed.

It was ten before the party started to sound like a party. Julia lay in bed reading, thinking of her boss's chest, and his almost too hairy legs, which looked like they weren't his just because the rest of him was so smooth. She wondered why he felt so comfortable getting undressed in front of her, even though he wasn't really undressed. It probably had more to do with the general pace of his life where things just needed to be done quickly.

Time was money, after all, so they said!

It got loud, and then it didn't. Loud again and then deathly quiet. Julia was curious about just what could be going on, but she quickly dismissed it. This had nothing to do with her, and as long as she just did her job, she didn't foresee any problems. She fell asleep thinking of what mess awaited her tomorrow.

And what a mess it was.

If she thought partying was reserved for Fridays, too, she quickly learned that this was not the case. Monday and Friday were interchangeable. Wednesday and Saturday may as well have been the same day. And the rest of the week was also fair game too.

She'd worked for Duwayne Jones for two months when she finally settled into the unpredictable nature of the job. But the parties were the most exciting part of the job, even though she never attended a single one. The rest of her job, while excessive, was rather boring. So Julia, *innocent, naive Julia* decided to play a game to make the job just a little more exciting. She cleaned his bedroom, leaving her underwear in his drawer, taking some of his...

CHAPTER TWO

*I*f he noticed, he didn't say anything. Duwayne Jones was young, by billionaire standards, 40, and *Autumn in Toronto* good looking, so all the sex he was having was expected. Since Julia started leaving her underwear in his bedroom, a very shortsighted joke on her part she was soon to find out, he'd brought seven women home. So Julia cleaned up after seven trysts, that she knew of. It really wasn't surprising that he didn't notice her undies, therefore, and she really was running out.

"Is the water pressure okay in your shower," he asked, about three months in. He was wrapped in a towel, making a smoothie in the kitchen, Julia just having walked in.

"It's perfect, she said, tying her apron around her waist and putting the many glasses on the counter in the dishwasher.

"Good..."

When he walked back upstairs, she saw the reason for his question. Every piece of underwear she'd left in his room was in a neat pile near the machine. There was a note on them, and she started to panic. He'd probably thought that she was using his shower. This was good. But why did she leave the underwear in his drawers? She wondered why he would think she'd done this as she picked up the note and turned it over slowly.

"If you want to ask me something, please, feel free..."

The smiley face at the end of this one sentence was unexpected. It did calm her down somewhat, even though she still had no idea what he thought she thought by doing this. She knew that she would need to explain herself, but she just wasn't ready. She would just need to avoid him for the rest of the day, or however long it took for her to be ready. Julia heard him coming back down the stairs, so she slipped into her courtyard.

"See you later, *Jules*..." he shouted from the kitchen before making his way quickly out the house.

Jules, she thought, wondering how they'd gotten here so quickly. Just yesterday, she was Julia. And he had already found all the undergarments, so this probably had nothing to do with this level of familiarity. If his intention was to *mind fuck* her, then it was working. She was well and truly coming undone, so much so that she really couldn't focus on her work today.

She started in his bedroom and found herself looking for stray garments that she knew she wouldn't find there. She'd barely finished when the phone was ringing downstairs, the first time since she'd started working there, in fact.

"Please drop the suit in my closet at the cleaners; I'm going to need it on the weekend!"

"Uhm, which one," she asked, nervous as soon as she heard it was him.

"Navy... It's standing alone, the only one in a cover!"

She still held the phone long after he had hung up. Why

would he not just ask her? Why did he insist on playing this new and uncomfortable game with her? Yes, she started it, she knew, but it was really just a joke, just to get rid of her boredom. It was to see if he would squirm, finding unfamiliar underwear in his drawers.

Just how observant was he, as a lover, she wondered suddenly. She was asking herself a series of questions, the answers of which were really none of her business. She asked them anyway, really wanting to know, suddenly. He was good looking and sexy as all hell. He looked very *capable*, and she wondered just how capable he actually was.

The absolutely consuming thoughts of Duwayne Jones kept her occupied until a little after five. She was in the kitchen when he arrived home, too early, and for just the second time, he caught her completely by surprise. She was lost in thought, clutching a cup of cold coffee.

"It's after five, you know," he said, pulling his tie off and unbuttoning his shirt all the way down.

"Huh," she said, trying again in vain to hide her surprise.

"Wine works better than coffee, *after five,*" Duwayne said.

He was already pouring both of them a glass. He handed it to her, took the cup, and put it on the counter. He was looking at her in an *unfamiliar, too familiar* way that made her feel like running away. There was nowhere to escape to, though.

"I liked the purple ones," he said.

Oh God, she thought. He was about to address it, and she was just not ready. She took a deep breath, sipped the wine she had no intention of drinking, and smiled. He smiled back at her and sipped his own wine.

"I am so sorry," she said. "It was a stupid joke that I really hadn't thought through!"

"Dammit..." he said and sipped his wine some more, slowly.

Julia didn't understand what he meant, so she just drank her own wine silently. She was watching him out of the corner of her eye, hoping that he would be the one to take his wine elsewhere and leave her to process her embarrassment. He had no intention of going anywhere, though, it seemed.

Duwayne was also looking at her, but not in the stolen way she was. He was really looking, taking in all of her. Julia was beautiful, leggy. And Duwayne, while he had a natural inclination towards redheads, was finding her extremely attractive now. He'd found her attractive from the moment he'd met her, but until she played this trick on him, he'd really never thought of her that way.

Theirs was supposed to be a professional relationship, which meant that all he expected of her was what she'd been doing, in fact. She worked hard, and she worked well. And she never passed any sort of judgment on any of the things she'd witnessed in his house.

Julia also never complained. She just got on with what she needed to do, and this was quite different from his previous help. He knew he was a bit messy, a bit much, and he hadn't expected her to make it passed the three-month mark. But she had, and this had something if not everything to do with the fact that this was her first job, he knew.

"Take that off," he said, pointing at her apron. Duwayne poured them both another glass of wine, and he walked out into her courtyard. She followed him and sat opposite him at the table two chairs that were there for her to relax after a long day's work or to enjoy her morning coffee in private. She took the apron off after she'd sat down, which made it funny to watch.

"So, what color," he asked.

"Excuse me," she said, unsure.

"Your panties... What color are they?" Duwayne asked seriously.

"I'm not sure," she said, and still sitting, she proceeded to take her panties off with her eyes closed, and then she held them out in front of her.

CHAPTER THREE

*S*he realized what she had done too late. Duwayne bent towards her and took the underwear from her with his mouth. She opened her eyes as he stood up, the white lace dangling from his mouth. He undid his belt, dropped his pants. His underwear was also white, tight briefs that hugged his enormous bulge. Julia thought of closing her eyes, but she couldn't. Instead, she just drank every drop of wine from her glass.

Then Duwayne smiled at her and pulled his underwear off. "Now we're even," he said, letting the panties fall from his mouth so that now, he too could finish his wine. They just watched each other now, nobody making any sudden moves. This really had escalated quite quickly.

Julia was the first to do something, her attempt to save Duwayne the embarrassment he was clearly not feeling. She stood up, unbuttoned her uniform, and took her bra, strapless, off. "Now we're even," she said.

He smiled broadly. He hadn't thought she would be this open to anything, but now that it was clear that she was, he couldn't hide his enthusiasm. His erection formed quickly, and it looked every bit like Julia thought it might when she had wondered about it. He took his shirt off and came around the table to stand in front of her and help her out of her uniform.

Both of them naked now, he picked her up off the ground, Julia wrapping her legs around his waist. Her breasts on his chest, they kissed, sharing the taste of the beautiful red they'd both just enjoyed.

Duwayne looked at her open door. He thought of taking her into the room, close and convenient, but thought against it. He wouldn't do that to her. He wouldn't reduce her to a stolen tryst in the servants quarters never to be spoken about again. His mouth on hers, he walked them back into the kitchen.

He placed her on the counter by the sink. He pulled her legs open, towards himself, and planted his face between her legs. He sent his tongue deep into her and inhaled hard. She smelled as delicious as she tasted. He let his tongue sit inside her for a while, enjoying the taste and the scent, before he started to move his thick tongue in and out of her. Duwayne was a master at what he was doing, and Julia lost her mind.

She was cumming hard and fast. It was unexpected but necessary. She hadn't been naked with a man in a minute, and so this really was a long time coming. Her flow went directly into his mouth, and he lapped up every drop.

"Yum fucking yum..." he said, lifting her off the sink and carrying her easily up the stairs.

He walked them into his bedroom and through it, to the bathroom. He stepped into his massive shower, still holding Julia up easily. Holding her against him with just one hand, he used the other to open the tap, preset so that he knew the temperature would be acceptable. It was.

Now he placed her down carefully, and Julia put herself

on her knees. Duwayne leaned back against the wall and bent his legs slightly to give her access to the parts of him she wanted. She took him into her mouth immediately and started to work on him with just her mouth almost as expertly as he had just worked on her.

"Yes... Yes... Yes..." he said.

She just sucked on him slowly, enjoying the precum trickling from his massive tip.

She was out of her depth. There was just too much going on around her so that she couldn't concentrate on what she was doing. Fortunately for her, Duwayne was actually a very observant lover, and he pulled himself from her mouth just so that he could reposition them so that the water wasn't falling directly on her face.

Now she was in her element.

Julia moved her lips up and down the sides of his thickness. Then she swirled her tongue around and around on and over his head before taking him into her mouth a millimeter at a time. Her tongue and teeth moved on every disappearing inch of him so that he felt like he was inside her already. It felt like anything but her mouth.

"Wow," he said when he hit the back of her throat. He held her head gently and held it in place. He thrust into her mouth ever so slightly just to settle in her completely, letting out a very loud exhale.

Duwayne pulled himself from her mouth as slowly as he had gone in, and then her tongue was swirling again around his head. Then, again, he was slowly going into her mouth, driving himself into her now, his hand on her head. He moved in and out of her mouth at a steady pace, his eyes on her face, her eyes closed. He wasn't close in any way, enjoying the act, loving the journey, no real urgency to get to the destination.

The shower on him directly *stayed* his orgasm so that he

could just enjoy the mouth he was occupying. She had her eyes open now, watching him watching her. She settled him deep in her throat once more, let it linger, and then pulled him from her completely. She got onto her feet, and he turned them so that Julia was against the wall now.

Again they were kissing, his hands all over her. She lifted one leg and wrapped it around his leg, bracing herself up so that she could grind her *happy place* against his *happy place*. There really was no rush between them, so that they both just rubbed up against each other hard.

Then Duwayne turned her around and was running his thickness between her cheeks. He had no intention of going in, enjoying this play. He rubbed his head against her rear entry point, pressed in a little, not trying to go in, just teasing. When his head started to make entry, though, he had to regroup quickly, about to get what he hadn't expected just yet, but now that *it was happening*...

Julia was holding her breath. She also hadn't expected this so soon, but now that it was happening, there was nothing she could do. She wanted him inside her, and exactly what inside her meant didn't really matter. She stayed completely still, trusting that he would know what to do and, more importantly, *how to do it.*

At almost the same millimeter by millimeter pace she had taken him into her mouth, he fed her ass, slowly. He couldn't rush this. He got a quarter of the way in and pulled out, going in again immediately before she snapped completely shut in protest. Then again, just a quarter inside her, he was thrusting, slowly. He tried for more, and she gave way, easily, taking half and then three-quarters of him inside herself. With just these two thirds, he went in and out of her, reaching around and into her with two of his fingers.

"You are... *Fantastic*..." He said this as he pushed his fingers all the way inside her and pushed her back onto himself so that every inch of him was inside her. He did not move now, except for his fingers. His intrusion was met with massive resistance so that he knew he needed to give her a very necessary moment...

CHAPTER FOUR

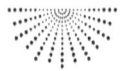

$\mathcal{T}$hen his fingers were out of her, his hands on her hips. He wasn't so much moving her as he was just holding her in place. Duwayne was moving himself, all the way in, all the way out. She offered less resistance each time he went back inside her so that the reentry was always quicker.

Then he wasn't moving, pushing her instead back and forth on himself. The fit was snug; it was tight. It was every kind of wonderful, and Duwayne now closed his eyes. When he was thrusting in and out of her, pushing and pulling her onto himself, the destination started to appear in the distance. He couldn't cum now, though, not yet. There was just one good orgasm in him, he knew, so he had to make it count, especially if he wanted this to happen again.

And he definitely wanted this to happen again.

When he was once again pulling himself completely from her, his eyes were open. He watched himself disappear completely into her delicious tightness. Over and over again, Duwayne pulled himself all the way out of her just to make sure that he didn't shoot his load prematurely.

He couldn't wait anymore. The risk that he would blow was too much now, so that he had to stay out of her. He looked down at his throbbing cock, purple and angry, wanting nothing more than to be spitting into her now. Duwayne took several deep breaths, turning Julia around so that she was looking at him. He kissed her full on her lips, his fingers just playing with the outside of her for the moment. And then, just one, he went into her, all the way.

Julia eyed his chest, his nipples. But before she could take them into her mouth, his own mouth was on her ripe, full breasts. He sucked slowly, expectantly. It was so deliberate that Julia opened her eyes now and watched him sucking her tits, almost expecting them to expel some or other elixir.

"Wow," it was her turn to mouth what she was feeling. She tried to say something else, but his finger was again inside her, all the way. Then a second finger snaked inside her, and he was moving just these two deep in and almost all the way out. His mouth never left her nipples once, except to alternate between them, and he proceeded to bring her to a perfectly *plausible* orgasm.

It was plausible because while she wasn't sure she'd had one, it was easy to believe that she had. Hot goo flowed from deep inside her and over Duwayne's hand, his fingers still inside her. He kept fingering her, albeit slower now, until she was having another, more intense orgasm. This time there was no doubt, and she quivered as the fingers inside her stayed put but were not moving.

He lifted her off the ground again, and despite herself, she wrapped her legs around his waist. Despite himself, Duwayne went inside her, in the place his fingers just were, and he settled himself completely inside her. He held her up and didn't move her. He didn't move himself, just pushing her against the wall so that all of him was in all of her.

"This is awesome..." he said.

"It is," she said.

They were kissing again, not moving the parts of them where they were joined, mostly because any sudden moves could lead to a premature end for Duwayne.

He lifted and lowered her onto himself now. He couldn't resist, needing to feel her on himself. She went easily, light as a feather. He moved her with such ease you would think he was stronger than he actually was.

Julia's legs slid off his waist, but she didn't fall. Duwayne's grip on her was firm; he would not let her. The feeling of her on every part of him was too wonderful a sensation to lose.

Again he turned so that he was backed up against the wall now. Still, he moved her up and down on himself with ease. Up and down, up and then all the way down, all the way up and then completely down on himself. Duwayne was still rock solid, with no signs of dissipation. He knew he could go on like this for a while, as long as he stayed aware. But he knew that she might get tired, already having had several orgasms, probably one good one left inside her, maybe two.

"I don't want to cum..." he said, closing his eyes, sinking his mouth into her breasts again.

"Then don't," she said, not sure if she wanted him to now.

"I'm not sure I can hold out much longer," he said, pushing her up and down on him once more for good measure. Then he lifted her off himself completely and put her on the shower floor. He turned her to face away from him, and he washed her back. He let the waterfall over both of them for a while before he turned the tap shut.

They left the cubicle. Duwayne dried her off somewhat before running the towel over himself. He walked her to the bed, mounting her as soon as she was on her back. He went all the way inside her and waited. He kissed her for the longest time before he started thrusting completely into her.

He knew that this was it. He was going for gold now, and

there was absolutely no turning back. Duwayne had paid careful attention to her for a while, and now he needed to pay attention to himself. There was no way he could concentrate on anything else at this particular moment.

He went deep. He went so deep and hard that every single thrust seemed to nail her to the bed. She felt as though she were being pushed into the mattress and through it. In actual fact, this is exactly what was happening.

Julia just took breath after very deep breath. She let out short yelps each time he settled completely into her. Over and over, he delivered himself into her, and over and over, she let out sounds that made the whole scene quite comical. Nobody was laughing, though. There was absolutely nothing funny about the umpteenth orgasm Julia was having.

He wanted to say something to fill the moment with words that would distract her until he had gone over the edge. She was finished. She was tired and needed a break but couldn't ask. Julia knew that he would cum soon, but how soon wasn't clear now as over and over he rammed himself into her.

The grunts coming from him now made her feel better. She thought he was either mid-orgasm or very close. But he just kept going, harder and harder. It seemed or rather felt like he was going deeper. Julia dug into herself for a second wind. She dug deep for the strength she needed to see him over the cliff that was so close now he was moaning loudly.

Still nothing, though, for the longest time. Still no sign of an actual end despite everything about the situation saying that it was over.

CHAPTER FIVE

"*I*'m close," he said again, but she didn't believe him. She also couldn't believe that she was close to and then having another orgasm. The sweat came off her in buckets now, so that she looked like she just came out of the shower. Duwayne, too, was sweating profusely.

And then it finally happened. He fed himself into her uniformly, each stroke exactly the same as the one before. This is how he always orgasmed. And even though this was his first orgasm in Julia, even though she had no frame of reference for this, she knew that firstly, it was over, and secondly, she would have to take it just about as long as he needed to complete this ritual.

When he was done, well and truly done, he pulled himself out of her loudly. It made a sound that again lent an element of comedy to the situation, but she wasn't laughing. Julia hadn't expected that it would be quite like this. Every moment of it was magnificent, but now that it was done, she couldn't move. She couldn't speak, couldn't laugh. She could hardly breathe.

Duwayne wrapped himself in a towel and went downstairs to get them a drink. He just brought the bottle upstairs and poured them both a glass when he was lying back on the bed. She didn't take her glass, not yet. Julia was still unable to move, and so she just lay there, still on her back for a while before rolling over onto her stomach.

He ran his fingers lightly through the black hair that stuck to her, part shower, mostly sweat. He wanted to say something to her but knew that nothing he said now would speed up her recovery. So he just sat there, sipping his wine and touching her hair.

After a while, she started to move slowly. She brought herself to sitting, still saying nothing as she sipped her wine. Duwayne rubbed his fingers across her back. She moaned and then looked at him, everything that had just happened still heavy in her eyes.

"Are you okay," he asked eventually.

"I'm not sure, " she answered honestly.

"Did I hurt you," he asked, needing to know.

She seemed to think about this for a while. He searched her eyes for the answer that just wasn't falling from her lips. "Of course not," she said eventually.

He smiled...

They had the rest of the wine before falling asleep in each other's juices. They had nowhere to be, not really, so they both fell asleep quite comfortably. Julia slept as though it was not her boss's bed. Duwayne slept the way you'd expect a man who'd just performed the way he ha would.

He woke up twice, once to go to the bathroom, once just because he *started*. He was disoriented the second time, and only when his eyes fell on Julia, who was sleeping silently away from him, did he remember where he was and with whom. He watched her in the darkness, surprised by his sudden arousal. He had always been a one orgasm man, but now here he was quickly sporting another massive *I want inside this woman* erection.

He knew he couldn't wake her, though, not for this, not for anything. He just hoped that she would be willing to let him have another go come morning...

* * *

THE SUN SHONE into the room brightly, illuminating Julia, whose mouth was working up and down Duwayne's morning wood. He was still asleep so that when he did start to stir, he thought for a moment that he might be dreaming. He lay back and closed his eyes, letting her do what it was obvious she really wanted to be doing right now.

"Good morning to you too..." he said when he realized this was not a dream.

She responded by settling him throat deep five or six times, her eyes on his eyes.

He just let her suck on him the way she wanted for as long as she wanted. She really seemed to be enjoying herself, and after what he had put her through the night before, she deserved this moment. Julia's mouth stayed on him until he exploded, a massive eruption coating the back of her throat.

She swallowed, *of course*.

Then she was on him.

Julia guided his now semi-hardon into herself. She sat on top of him and started to move in easy back and forth rocking movements. He was still half asleep, so was she, so it was easy and dreamy and absolutely everything morning sex should be. Duwayne kept opening and closing his eyes, still not completely convinced that he wasn't dreaming.

As he hardened inside her again, she had to wake up now.

The monster she'd created herself had proven itself last night, and now, she just needed it to be easy. There was nothing light about this situation, mind you, but with Julia in the driver's seat, it seemed to take a gentler slant.

She rode him slowly, steadily. Again the absence of any rush was obvious. They both just seemed content with the journey. The destination was inevitable; they both knew a conclusion.

Duwayne mouthed something, but the words were not audible. Julia was sure he hadn't used any real words, in fact. Now she did laugh. She laughed loudly so that he opened his eyes and looked at her.

"What are you saying," she asked him.

"I have no idea... What did you hear?"

She didn't answer. She moved in wide circles on him now, pulling him in every direction. There was nothing that he needed to do. There was nothing that he could do, in fact, except to just lie there and let her do whatever she wanted, however, she wanted.

What she wanted felt amazing. She brought him so close that he thought he would burst or implode if he didn't cum. But then he didn't, stayed by the power of the thighs working on him. Again she brought him close, only to send him back a few paces. She controlled him this way until she was so close that at any minute she would herself explode. She worked him up to a final frenzy and then brought them both crashing down to the bed first, then through it and through to the center of the earth.

Duwayne just looked at her. She looked extremely proud of herself. She was extremely proud of herself. She wasn't looking at him now, tipping the empty glass into her mouth. He knew she deserved a morning drink, but he couldn't move, not yet.

"I'll get it, don't worry. You don't move..."

When she came back with another full bottle of wine, he took his hand to his ear, pretending to be on the phone.

"That was your boss. He says you don't need to come in today..."

ABOUT THE AUTHOR

Tala Melton is an emerging erotica author of naughty maids and their billionaire bosses.

Readers: I want to expand a few of the stories to see where the characters can be explored further. If there are any of the stories that you would like to read more about again, I'd love to hear from you!

Visit my blog at Tala Melton Blog
Join my newsletter for free exclusive previews Tala Melton Newsletter
Follow me on Twitter at Tala Melton Twitter
Like my page on Facebook at Tala Melton FB

Sign up for Free Stories from Xplicit Press Authors
Xplicit Press Updates
Like Xplicit Press on Facebook
Follow Xplicit Press on Twitter

MORE NAUGHTY MAID STORIES BY TALA MELTON

Naughy Maids and The Dirty Billionaire Bosses